Happily Never After Midnight
And Other Bedtime Lies

By: M.M. Anderson

2015 Published by Little Shop of Writers

Library of Congress Copyright

@ 2014 by M.M. Anderson

www.littleshopofwriters.org

This book is dedicated to Ian and Mia, my finest creations, and to my best buddy.

AN AUSPICIOUS ASSORTMENT OF WHIMSICAL WORKS
For Grown Ups

TABLE OF CONTENTS

ANGELIC PERSUASION

A pretty petite angel dressed in scant more than white wings sat upon the sooty skyscraper sill watching the minuscule masses below.

"Insects," she declared. "Anxious ants, racing to a spitty spec of candy."

"You're right!" came a roaring reply from the cornerstone. "From this height humans do resemble—" The orator paused mid-sentence. "I speak?"

"Which beast addresses me?" the angel called. She scanned the menagerie of stone animal effigies that adorned the First Trust Bank building façade.

"It is Lion."

The angel didn't acknowledge Lion's response immediately. Instead, she skipped and shimmied along the razor-sharp ridge, as nimble, lithe, and carefree as the wind. A finale pirouette placed her beneath Lion's perch.

"Ah, there you are," the angel purred, sounding as if she'd come to the end of a lengthy search. "You are ever so handsome and I admire the forceful rumble of your roar."

The weathered beast's breast swelled with pride. "I am attractive," he said. It was a question as well as a statement and it stirred something deep within him. The marble base below Lion's paws began to tremble.

"Come here," the angel requested. She held out her hand.

Lion detached his maned mass from the cornerstone, stretched his appendages, and pounced onto the long ledge below.

The angel brushed a clump of pigeon guano from Lion's quarried coat and patted his head. Lion recalled the only other instance he had been touched, by the stonecutter who'd crafted him many decades before.

"Ever so lonely," she whispered.

Lion couldn't be sure if the angel was referring to his thought, or making a personal remark. Before he had the opportunity to inquire she slipped past him and began another dance display, this time while chanting a haunting dirge. "*Domine Jesu, dimitte nobis debita nostra.*"

Lion listened and observed. The angel embodied exquisite beauty. She had a fair face, ginger ringlets framing rosy porcelain cheeks. Her diminutive physique was trim, firm, and agile. The beast sensed the angel to be tender, passionate, and ladylike. Yet, there was something aloof and childish about her too.

"*Salva nos ab igne inferni.*"

"What are you singing?" he asked.

"A prayer," she giggled, as if his question had been silly. The angel crouched before Lion. She placed her lips near his ear and continued the enchanting tune.

Lion shut his eyes and rested his chiseled chin upon her knee. He understood none of the words, but the mesmerizing melody engulfed him in a warmth he knew was love.

"*Perduc in caelum omnes animas, praesertim eas, quae misericordiae tuae maxime indigent.*" The angel's song ended. She wandered towards the flagpole and gazed up at a row of windows. "Lion, you have not asked the reason I am here."

Up to this point, Lion hadn't wondered. Nor had he considered why this was the first time he'd constructed a thought, spoken, or detached from his base.

"Waiting for a human," the angel answered herself.

"A human?" Lion repeated. "This is an unlikely place to encounter one."

No sooner had Lion's words been uttered then a pane above them shattered, sending glass shards showering through the air. A blue blazer was draped over the jagged opening and a middle-aged man dressed in business attire climbed out onto the shelf.

The angel smiled.

"I'm not going to prison!" he professed, brow beaded with perspiration, legs trembling. The man plastered himself against the building façade and took two steps towards the unadorned flagpole. "I'd rather jump twenty-six floors!"

Twenty-seven," the angel corrected, without the slightest hint of concern in her voice.

The man startled and lost what fragile footing he had. In an instant he was no longer standing along the building edge, but dangling from it, grasping for life.

The angel flapped her wings and floated above him. "Twelve seconds traveling until you reach pavement."

"Help me, please," the man begged, swinging his lanky legs in an effort to return them to the limestone ledge. "Who are you?"

"Guardian angel." She placed her tiny toes upon his clenched fingers.

"I, I wasn't really going to commit suicide," the man stammered, his hands quivering, nail beds turning white. "Creative business deal. Investors found out their money's gone."

"You have come here by your own free will," the angel affirmed.

"No. It's my secretary's fault. She called the board."

"Are you seeking forgiveness?" The angel struck a bargaining tone.

"Forgive me for falling! Now get your feet off my hands. Pull me up!"

The angel folded her arms and waited.

The man grunted and managed to swing one shoe back onto the shelf. "Please!" His wide eyes beseeched her. "I'm a banker but I was once an alter boy."

"Do you believe in one God Almighty, creator of Heaven and Earth, all that is seen and unseen, with life everlasting, amen?"

"Whatever's going to save me!"

"Very well," the angel replied, stepping aside. "Trust in your faith and let go."

"Let go?" the man cried.

"God helps those who help themselves. Your hands cannot grasp any longer."

The banker's tired trembling fingers lost their tenuous hold. For a moment his rigid contorted body balanced on the sill.

Lion's courage rose. The stone beast attempted to sacrifice his own safety and intervene, but found himself once again frozen in place. He could do nothing but stare in silent suspense.

The balancing moment ended.

While peering over the building ledge the angel counted backwards from twelve. "Eleven, ten, nine, eight, seven…"

Down, down the banker descended, until his flailing body landed like a porous sack of chunky vegetable chowder alongside a double-parked taxicab.

"The way I feel about humans," she confessed. "It is a wonder I became an angel."

THE END

FORTY WINKS

Staff pointing and dutiful demeanor unyielding, Owl directed his grumbling lumbering ward towards a slumberful slab of stone. "Forty winks, big fellow."

The beast halted mid tracks. "Why?" He crossed his formidable furry arms and furrowed his horn-adorned brow. "Me not tired."

"Certainly, you must be exhausted," Owl replied through a restrained yawn. He did not relish another night of limited but persistent conversation regarding the inevitable. It had been a particularly long and arduous day, wrangling and amusing the creature who reminded Owl of a mammoth mosquito, one that was not easily discouraged from inflicting pain and annoyance.

"Me want story," began the beast's well-rehearsed nightly plea bargain. "Not go to sleep." His visage, however, begged to differ, jowls limp and lids lethargic.

"Very well." Owl countered with an innocuous abbreviated fairytale. "Once upon a time. Far, far away. Happily ever after. The end." He patted the ledge. "Bed."

"Me no like that story." Beast looked away and huffed.

"Suit yourself." While Owl contemplated his next nanny gambit, a familiar wily winged woman appeared, wearing only a twinkle in her eyes and carrying a gilded journal. "Hello." She waved her fingertips and tossed her tied tousled locks. "I've written Minotaur a bedtime tale, a little epic poem."

"That's an oxymoron! Go away!" Owl screeched. "Minotaur doesn't need any more distractions. He has himself and that's plenty!"

"Me want story!" The beast snorted and pawed like Taurus ready to charge.

"Unwise to rile him!" Owl scolded as he fluttered out of Minotaur's petulant path.

"Music and poetry soothe the savage soul." The feathered femme opened her writing book to a marked page. "May I?" Her batting baby browns beckoning the raptor's permission.

"If you must," Owl acquiesced.

She cleared her throat. "This piece is entitled, *Goodnight Minotaur*."

"That me!" chuckled the man-bull. He ceased his bedtime rebellion and struck an attentive position of repose.

Owl settled on the beast's bottom, back exposed to the storyteller, privately pleased that for a change someone else would lull them into Dreamland.

The poet commenced reading in a sing-song voice from her personal volume of verse:

Tread softly for Minotaur sleeps
If awakened he thunders and heaps
Fierce destruction across the ancient Grecian isle of Crete

"Me monster!" Minotaur rocked back and forth on his hocks with delight.

Quick talon reflex prevented Owl from jiggling off his animated derrière perch.

"Ouch, feet hurt me." Minotaur rubbed his rump.

"Then stop wiggling." Owl made himself comfortable once again.

She continued:

Once captured inside a Labyrinth cage
Athens paid annum tribute to the hellion's potent rage
Seven lads devoured and virgins ravished upon his bloody stage

The toned temptress enunciated and animated the last stanza with deliberate verve.

"More, more!" Drool pooled in the corners of Minotaur's quivering mouth as he writhed his erect Cyclops muse against the firm marble.

"Enough, sly siren!" Owl shouted. He snatched the book from her grasp. "That is not a bedtime story; it's an aphrodisiac!"

"Owl, give my poems back, this instant!" She fluttered across Minotaur, bare breasts brushing against his damp snout an instant before her female fault came to a halt above the beast's flared nostrils. The moist musky scent triggered a lascivious frenzy.

"Down boy!" Owl tossed the volume aside and latched onto Minotaur's thrashing tail. "Fly fast before he eats you alive!"

She dodged the savage's bullish charge, but Owl wasn't as fortunate. Minotaur's whipping tail sent the small stout sentry head-first into stone with a mighty THUNK. He slid to the ground, a pulverized pile of limp feathers.

The beast ceased stampeding. Head hung in remorse, he plodded over to where Owl lay motionless. "Me bad."

"Hush." She placed her ear against the battered bird's chest. "His heart is still beating."

"Forty winks?" Minotaur asked.

She nodded. "Forty winks." The pretty poet retrieved her poems. "Come with me."

"Story time?"

"Yes, Daedalus has constructed another wooden cow." She took the beast's hand. "I'll read to you again before crawling inside…"

THE END

THE CREATION

Eve reclined on a mossy ridge watching her charges cavort in the lush emerald garden that was Eden. Elephants and emus, gorillas and gnus, fanciful feathered parrots and colorful crested chameleons were among the creatures present in her view. There was much delightful nothing to do in Paradise, no foraging or migration, no predators hunting prey. Instead, God made abundant manna available to feast upon throughout Eden's never-ending day.

With stomachs satisfied, the beasts took advantage of infinite opportunity for preening, coitus, and other joyful couples' play. Eve, however, had no human companion, no species mate with whom to groom or indulge her carnal cravings. Penetration being the mother of fenestration, Eve had become rather adept at satisfying herself with phallic vegetation while partaking vicariously in the many and varied wild acts of animal foreplay and copulation.

Some species stimulated Eve's libido more than others. The bonobos' insatiable reliance on fornication as a mode of salutation, dispute resolution, and celebration, paired with their homosexual, oral, and incest dalliances put the the plucky primates at the top of Eve's titillating voyeur list, while hippopotami earned the dubious distinction of finishing last. In fact, if in the vicinity when a male river horse approached a female, Eve turned the other cheek and promptly sought cover.

In nature it is customary for an aroused male hippopotamus to position himself where a potential mate can clearly see him. Upon gaining her undivided attention the randy bull commences defecating himself, while at the same time urinating. Obviously, a duet of feces and urine alone would scarcely impress a selective hippo cow (for any male creature can soil himself), therefore, to prove worthy of a roll in the riverbank reeds, the hippo suitor would then spin his turd-shaped tail like a propeller, slinging the fetid moist mixture, which was, apparently, quite seductive to the observing female.

Eve shunned the rank image from her visual memory and commenced reminding her body about the benefits of singlehood when the Maker appeared. "Hello, God," Eve said.

"Hello, my daughter. Pleased to see you enjoying yourself," God replied. "I have been concerned that Woman is my only creation without a mate. Despite the plethora of flora and fauna here in Eden, I know you are often quite lonely."

"True." Eve set down her bruised zucchini. "I fantasize about having a partner."

God touched Eve's delicate hand. "Then I shall make for you a suitable mate. He will be called Man."

"Man!" Eve did not contain her excitement. "Please, I want to know all about him!"

"Very well," God continued. "To begin with, Man will be a product of your recent pondering. Like bonobo, Man will crave copulation for its own sake, yet akin to hippopotamus he will be impressed with his bodily waste production and odors. So much so that Man will go out of his way to share his scents, sounds, and excretions with Woman."

Eve did not know whether to wretch or rejoice.

"Do not fret, my child. There is more to Man," God assured. "With proper training he will fulfill your every nubile notion. Where you are physically fragile, Man is strong. He will often forget, so you can learn to always remember. But most important, the trials and tribulations of dealing with Man's excreta, pride, ego, and desire to possess noisy, shiny objects will prepare you to one day bare and raise many human offspring."

"Offspring?" Eve rubbed her taut belly. She had not considered the fruits of mating. "Is there anything else I should know about Man?"

"Only this," God said. "I will make Man on one condition, that you keep a secret."

"Why a secret?" Eve had never before been asked by God to withhold truth.

God sighed. "In accordance with Man's arrogance and penchant to be in charge, he will naturally believe he was made first. To learn otherwise would be a crushing blow to Man's self-esteem. Do you promise, Eve, to guard this secret between us, woman to woman?"

"I do…"

THE END

SWAN'S WAKE

Leda stood beside her ailing grandmother's wheelchair that faced the hospice garden lake. A gaggle of snowy geese and a lone trumpeter swan paddled with enthusiasm across late afternoon titian shadows towards the tree-lined shore where a dinner bucket of cracked corn and stale bread was being served by a grinning groundskeeper.

The mid March weather was more lion than lamb. Leda fastened her overcoat. "Sure you don't prefer to go inside and watch today's sunset from the observatory?" She draped a knitted lap blanket over Grandmother's frail fingers. "Might catch—" Leda stopped herself.

"Catch my death of cold?" Grandmother replied. "Something's going to kill me. May it happen sooner rather than later." She removed her tiny tissue-clenching fist from its cover and coughed a hunk of black goo into the wadded ball of cotton. "I am ready to die and move into a new body."

Leda tried to think of a positive retort while privately praying that Grandmother wouldn't ask her to dispose of the soiled tissue. All she could muster was, "You'll be an angel."

"Hardly," Grandmother chuckled. "Holy wings are reserved for sweet souls. Except to you, dear Leda, I have been cruel and cross and spiteful most of my life without a moment's remorse. For penance, my soul will enter an animal when I pass."

In Leda's astute thirteen years she had witnessed Grandmother fouling more than a few family functions with her fierce temper and outrageous antics. She often reminded Leda of a monkey, on the one hand diminutive and adorable, while on the other a vengeful prankster.

When Father objected unsuccessfully to Grandmother's permanent relocation to their home and guest room, the old woman countered by assuming laundry duties and taking it upon herself to sew shut the traps of his undershorts. The mending caused Father abject embarrassment as he stood beside a trio of office subordinates in the men's lavatory after having consumed his morning quart of coffee. To date Father has not been able to shed his acquired work moniker: *The Urinator*.

Grandmother pointed her gnarled index finger at the majestic bird dining beneath the weeping willows. "First, I will be a swan. Elegant and graceful, like a dancer. Yet, fierce as a street fighter when threatened."

Leda imagined a shimmering soul floating into the black beaked beast. It gave her comfort to think Grandmother could somehow live on after death.

After a pensive pause the matriarch continued. "Your talent comes from me. Until the war stole childhood, I too studied ballet. My dream was to perform Swan Lake."

"I had no idea you were a ballerina." Leda wondered what else she would never know about her grandmother.

"Yes, and after I am a swan I shall shift my soul into another human being, one that won't mind the temporary intrusion. Before reincarnating again, I wish to sample many different perspectives." Grandmother's faded watery eyes brightened. "Perhaps I will share form with a circus clown, preferably a dwarf or midget, some mischievous court jester who can juggle a quartet of balls and possesses *carte blanche* when it comes to goosing onlookers and rattling eardrums with obnoxious horn blasts."

As if on cue, the evening meal siren sounded, sending the feasting flock into a fit of flight and putting an end to visiting hours.

Leda envisioned a mental movie circus scenario and smiled as she maneuvered the rigid metal rolling chair across a grassy twilit lawn to the cafeteria building where Grandmother attended her last supper.

****

Leda and her parents greeted friends and distant family members who came to pay their respects to the woman who slumbered eternally inside the shut wooden box adorned by a foreign flag and a framed photograph that captured younger years.

After kneeling beside the casket and muttering a prayer or two, most mourners signed the guest registry and deposited a card on the perimeter table before taking a seat in the solemn space provided by hospice. Leda scanned the small sea of expressionless faces and wondered whether or not each of them had been touched by Grandmother's bedeviling.

If any persons hadn't, they soon would be.

"Oh my gosh!" Mother gasped, catching sight of a white bird waddling into the wake.

"A swan!" Leda declared in excited disbelief.

Forty eyes focused on the feathered visitor that seemed to be surveying the crowd while web-footing its way closer to the casket.

"Shoo!" Father shouted, snatching a long unlit candle from its holder and brandishing it like a sword in the direction of the curious creature. "Out of here, this instant!"

"Please, don't hurt her!" Leda stepped between her father and the bird she was certain must be Grandmother making good on her promise. "The swan only wants to know who came to pay their respects."

The animal appeared to nod in agreement.

"See?" Leda said.

"Nonsense," Father scoffed , stepping out from behind his daughter and shuffling close enough to poke the bird's breast twice with the tip of his wax saber. However, he did not get the opportunity to jab thrice before a furious display of flapping, hissing, and honking commenced, prompting mourners to scurry for safety. Father attempted to follow their room-exiting lead but the swan was quite a bit quicker. She attacked with a blinding flurry of nips and pecks, launching Father stumbling and tumbling off balance through a vacated row of seats and into the registry table, sending sympathy cards sailing like confetti through the incensed air. If not for the perfect aim of the hospice groundskeeper's net upon the angry pen, Father's retreating bottom would have been pâté.

"So sorry," the workman apologized after he subdued the big bird. "Had her since she was a cygnet. Never seen this sort of behavior, and I never seen her leave the lake to attend a wake before, either." He hoisted the still sack over his shoulder.

"What are you going to do with her?" Leda stroked the swan's side through the nylon netting. "Not the poor animal's fault Father attacked first with a candlestick."

"How do you recall I received this gash?" Father stammered as he pointed to small scrape on his left hand, caused when it connected with the corner of an aluminum folding chair. "That bird is vicious!"

"Putting her back in the lake where she belongs. Won't bother you again," the groundskeeper assured. "Promise I'll keep an eye on her."

"What about me?" Father once again noted his injury. "This cut could become infected."

"I'll show you to the infirmary on my way out," the workman offered.

Leda followed the trio into the vestibule and watched in somber silence as her father and grandmother headed down the hall. Yes, she was sure it was Grandmother.

"Leda," Mother called from the viewing room.

Leda returned to find her mother and another guest on their knees collecting the scattered cards, most of which were addressed to *The Family of* or *In Loving Memory of,* Grandmother's full name following. There was one exception.

"This is for you." Mother held out a bright blue envelope that was marked in a familiar stylized script, ***To My Leda***.

Leda tore the seal without hesitation. There was no condolence note within, instead the item Leda found made her squeal. "I knew it!" She held up the card stock contents: a single ticket to the circus.

THE END

STILL LIFE

Central Station was bustling with travelers shlepping satchels and sacks laden with token gifts and goodies to give upon arrival at holiday dinner destinations. In transit guests who had not made present purchases beforehand browsed and bought from rows of railway lobby sweets and souvenir stands.

Scented candles and a sage wreath, Catherine reviewed her hostess offerings while waiting patiently in a long line to make a personal purchase at *Le Chocolatier*. Imported candies were her favorite indulgence. Be that as it may, the frugal spinster only allowed herself the pricey pleasure of Belgian truffles covered in a bittersweet dusting of cinnamon, powdered sugar and coco once a year, when she ventured out of her still life in the city to her ancient auntie's obligatory November Thursday feast at the family farm.

"Milk, white, or dark?" the harried high schooler clerk asked. "One-pound, two-pounds, or six-piece sampler?"

"Dark. Half-dozen," Catherine replied. She reached into her worn wallet, removed three bills and exact coins. "No gift-wrap or bag necessary."

The attending teen appeared relieved not to labor or apply math skills. He handed her a pre-packaged purple-ribboned box and no change. "Happy holidays."

"Thank you." Catherine took two steps forward to allow the next customer counter access when she was jostled by an impatient commuter. The whack spun her in a circle and disoriented her wares. She had a peeved penchant to apprehend and scold the unapologetic perpetrator who was fast becoming one with the rushing crowd. Instead, the archival librarian took a calming breath, gathered her parcels, and found an empty spot on an occupied two-person waiting area bench beside a handsome middle-aged man. The only barrier preventing the travelers from touching was a bowed box of truffles. He flashed a friendly smile. She returned a polite nod, scooted left, and checked the terminal clock, thankful the 12:34 to Alexandria Junction would be boarding by and by.

When venturing out of her daily routine and comfort zones Catherine made it a point to keep a differential distance from others, not speak to or make eye-contact with male strangers, or any unfamiliar females dressed or behaving inappropriately. Not since her fiancé abruptly ended their decade-long engagement had Catherine felt the desire to mix or mingle. Yet, at this moment she was compelled to give the man on her right lingering glances. His dreamy blue eyes, salt and pepper hair, and mesmerizing matinee idol features resembled her ideal man, *Paul Newman...* A sudden surge of tingling fire flushed Catherine's cheeks and aroused her recessed feminine waters. For an amatory instant the solitary book worm was home, enjoying a randy moonlit fantasy flinted by D.H. Lawrence and oaky Chardonnay, but this time she wasn't alone, and it wasn't a cat's tail she imagined rubbing against bare skin beneath crisp sheets.

"Afternoon," he said.

"Good afternoon," Catherine stammered as she unfastened the purple bow and helped herself to a truffle, hoping the tasty treat would satisfy her previous precipitous urge to indulge in something sinfully creamy. The first bite of bitter confection made her moan.

The man watched, winked, and removed a candy from its ribbed paper container. "Dark chocolate is my favorite too."

Immodest illusions dissipated the instant Catherine observed with aghast an absolute stranger sampling her sweets without permission or invitation. *What nerve!*

Like theater popcorn, he ate the truffle and reached immediately for another. "Do you detect a hint of hickory and pepper?"

"I do not!" Catherine retorted. She grabbed a second chocolate and consumed it in a single chew and swallow.

The man chuckled. "I admire a woman who goes after what she wants." He removed a third candy before presenting her with the box. "Last truffle's yours."

That is the final straw! Catherine bolted off the bench. "I have tolerated enough insolence. That truffle certainly is mine, but you may have it, for I will not allow myself to be the recipient of token remains, ever again!" A flashing green light along the platform announced the train's pending arrival. Catherine gathered her bags and made pronounced haste towards the open doors without looking back. *Self-serving brute; men are all the same!*

Catherine's seven minutes of smoldering over shared chocolates was promptly put on hold when the conductor arrived to punch her boarding ticket. She checked both coat pockets. It wasn't there. *Purse?* No. *Wallet?* Not there either. Panic set in as she revisited every crevice, compartment, and corner, her hands shaking from embarrassment coupled with track turbulence. "I purchased a round-trip at the station."

The uniformed conductor steadied himself on the headrest of the empty seat beside Catherine as she rummaged. "No worries," he assured. "Probably fell into one of those totes. Catch you on the return." The conductor tipped his cap before exiting into the aft railcar.

Catherine was sure she hadn't placed the transfers in with her hostess gifts. However, search options were limited. She removed the decorative tissue-wrapped wreath and candle from their oversized satchel and placed them on the vacant seat. *That's funny?* Something else remained at the bottom of the big bag. She reached inside and pulled out a rectangular box bound with purple ribbon, a train ticket tangled in the folds. Catherine's stomach sank, releasing repeat remains of stolen sweet chocolatey hickory and pepper.

"Nearly made me miss this train," a man standing in the aisle declared.

"Huh?" Catherine looked up to see Paul Newman's twin holding a bowed box.

"Peace offering." He handed her the truffles. "Not sure what I did wrong back there," he wondered aloud. "But if there's still life like that inside you at our age, you're someone I want to know better..."

THE END

FINAL BLOW

Molan awoke, his throat parched, body beneath battered boards in a concealed cellar crevice devoid of light. The cacophony of crashing waves, howling winds, raging thunder, and warning bells were again silent. He supposed the cohorts had moved on without him.

The naked man grappling in the darkness had a history of stormy relationships, beginning with Snow. She was fresh falling when they met, a divine dusting of uncharted white. No man's footprints came before Molan's, no prior tracks to brush away or discern. He was captivated by Snow's beauty, blinding in daylight and bewitching when bathed in moon's azure glow. The maiden explorer recalled reveling in Snow's powdery drifts while she came, down, down, in heavy silence until Molan was so deep inside her he could venture no further, lust's avalanche.

Weeks, months accumulated; days grew longer. Snow aged. Her once firm mounds, slush. Soiled, barren, grey, her softness replaced by an icy veneer. Molan's sentiments thawed too. He craved youth, warmth. He sought Spring. Jealous Snow raged, retaliated with a final frosty vengeance. Limbs bowed to her wintery wrath. Molan turned his back on her, blanketed himself in the certainty that *this too shall pass*. It did. Snow's acquiesce left him free to be with another.

Molan's season with Spring began as a mild respite: colorful, fresh. Be that as it may, their gentle union soon dampened by frequent rains and Spring's middling moods, which vacillated between chilly and tepid. Molan tired of passivity. He craved fervor and focused his sights elsewhere. Spring cried a river when Molan left the nest for blazing Summer.

Molan and Summer had dinner under the bridge their first night together. The ensuing heat was immediate and intense. Summer was moist, steamy, relentless, and as scorching as the June solstice was long. By late August Molan was parched and lethargic, sucked dry. He took refuge in the shade. When he tried to move on, partake in Autumn's crisp russet harvest, Summer's Indian fire sparked and held the mature and bountiful would-be paramour at bay.

It was during the September stand off that Molan first learned of the Twisted Tempest. She was called Gale by some, Mariah by others. By every account she was a dominatrix force of nature. Molan's fickle interest was redirected, aroused.

The chase commenced, a perilous whirlwind across deserts and plains to the coast where she was forecasted. Curiosity fueled Molan's fantasy. *Could this tawdry temptress be as untamed as men claimed?*

Skies grew dark, hail fell, a deafening roar commenced. Gale appeared on the horizon, a fearsome funnel moving with unbridled haste, tumbling all in her path. Molan held steadfast, his reckless craving unwavering. She obliged, lashing him hard into submission. Molan cried out in pleasured pain. But the fiery pang passed too quickly. Like the delicious burn of wasabi, he hungered for another hot bite.

Gale had no geographic boundaries, no confining calendar. The pair traveled together on wild whim. Her innate brutality caused Molan to come to terms with his previous limits. Over and over he fell hard for her. The closer to death Gale blew him, the more alive he felt, alert and masculine in a cathartic role as willing whipping boy, strong and confident for the first time that he could withstand any assault. For perverse reasons of personal preservation and pride, Molan *needed* to hurt.

He became a servant of the storm, but not her only companion.

On occasion Gale partnered with another femme force of nature. Sandy? Katrina? Molan could not recall her name, only recent warnings. She was poised to leave a perfect wake of destruction in her path.

The storm chaser occupied an evacuated residence, awaiting the duo's onslaught. He passed time in the foyer with a forgotten feline, spotted white ginger, none too interested in the trespasser's presence. Molan disrobed before the hall mirror. He admired as he shed, a brawny glass reflection. Pain had begot gain. His scared calloused crusader swelled, an ardent urge to be weather-beaten by both inamoratas. *Ménage à trois*.

Shutters shook, rough rain pounded Rossini crescendos upon the tin roof. Cat headed for the cellar. The stormy symphony redirected Molan's attentions and summoned him outside. Beyond the transom he was greeted by a warm wet pelting. With arms open, lapping tongue, Molan consumed water salty sweet and plentiful. It pooled in his mouth, provoked his thirst to be blown by her in the ensuing shower.

Gale arrived at the scene.

Molan looked up to find Gale's circular opening overhead. The rotating cloud walls of her cavern made visible by blue bursts of lightning ricocheting within. The spectacle was accompanied by a loud hissing noise and an onset of warning bells sounding from a nearby church. Gale whirled forward. She shook the beach house, wrenched its roof away, and tossed it whole into the turbulent surf. A thunderbolt whizzed past Molan's head.

He sensed that their coupling had taken a different turn.

The storm chaser made flaccid haste back inside the topless bungalow, through rainy windswept hall, down dank cellar stairs, towards the furthest reaches of musty darkness. He crammed his wet nakedness into a cobwebbed cleft, as fractured floors and furious flood came, came, came upon him...

****

Molan awoke beneath battered boards in a concealed cellar crevice devoid of light.

He crawled free. There was neither ceiling nor sky above. Cat purring and candlelight flickering nearby beckoned investigation.

Molan recognized the spotted white ginger feline crouched casually upon a jute rug. "You were earlier in the foyer."

"Greetings," Cat replied. His crooked tail swiping back and forth, directing Molan's eyes to a pair of doors. "Choose a room you wish to enter."

Behind the first Molan encountered a scene similar to the one he had escaped, Gale and her typhoon companion desecrating the seaside town. A flailing faceless figure, pummeled by passing debris, clung to the remains of a battered bungalow and begged the sky for mercy. Molan slammed door one and hurried to the next.

Cat was unmoved.

The second door contained a disparate event, a man reclining upon a rock, an attractive nude woman on her knees, providing pleasure. The recipient man was, however, grotesque. His hair tangled in seaweed, skin scorched, scaly, bloated, as if electrocuted before being soaked in a brackish bath.

The twisted sight excited Molan.

"Whichever door selected, the person in that room shall exchange places with you," Cat explained. "For eternity."

Molan desired what was behind door number two.

"Very well." Cat entered the appointed room and brushed against the woman's shoulder. "You may leave now. I have found a replacement."

THE END

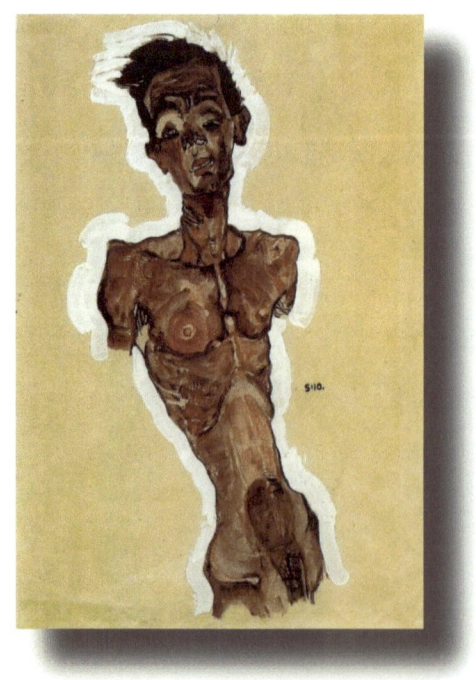

POND LOUGH

Cill Áirne perched upon Kerry's southwestern seacliff like a harbor hawk. Prior to designations and inhabitants she sprung forth from ancient volcanoes blanketed in ice. An expansive glacier, sole resident, receding, sculpting magnificent mounts later called Torc, Crohane, and Mangerton. Erosion moving massive boulder stone and gravel, carving sinuous passes between lush emerald peaks, Moll's Gap and the Gap of Dunloe. In addition to summits and dells, retreating frost thawed, forming deep dark *loughs*, Tir na N'og, and other peculiar watery proprietors of Irish myths and legends.

"The lough's haunted and it ain't got no bottom." Uncle Cecil gave his guests a glaring gander. "Should ye decide to go bathing, no venturing far from shore or them mischievous demons will be teaching a trespassing lesson not soon forgotten." The burley host downed a substantial swig of Guinness. "Any fella what doubts me word would also be fool enough to bolt 'is door with a boiled carrot when the devil came a calling." He wiped beer froth onto the back of his fleshy fist. "I speak the truth, no less."

"Aye, well, sometimes a right bit more." Aunt Bridget scooted her chair away from the table. "Quit repeating foolish legend, Cecil. There ain't no ghosts, ghouls, or banshees in that there watering pond." She gathered dirty dinner plates and made her way out of the room.

Uncle Cecil watched the kitchen door close before resuming his tale. "Last spring one a me cows waded in too deep while quenching her thirst, and a red-eyed fiend grabbed hold of Bessie's bell and dragged her beneath the blackness to hell. Ain't never found the carcass."

"Thought you sold that old Holstein?" Aunt Bridget questioned from beyond the swinging portal. "Enough. I said, no more filling our visitors' heads with stories about cow thieving pond demons."

"It's a lough, woman!" Uncle Cecil slammed his calloused palm like a judge's gavel against the oak tabletop.

Jacob jumped.

"Pond, lough, no matter, Cecil." Aunt Bridget returned with dessert. "You're giving this poor lad the jitters." She served four hearty slices of warm black currant tart topped with a dollop of fresh whipped cream. "Our niece and her fine new husband are probably regretting paying us a honeymoon visit."

Uncle Cecil mumbled an inaudible retort and scarfed in silence.

Aunt Bridget ate quietly as well.

Zaira and Jacob commented on the awkward deafening hush with finger touches and leg brushes behind shield of tablecloth.

"I don't find myself in the mood for pie seconds tonight, woman, on account a being called a liar in front of me family," Uncle Cecil announced after licking his plate clean. "Going to me office." He lumbered into the garden and lit a pipe.

"He'll be his jovial self tomorrow," Aunt Bridget assured, her cheery countenance returned. "I set extra towels in your room and fastened the shutter. Rest from the long journey and help yourselves to breakfast. Uncle Cecil and me will be making an early trip to Tralee. But we'll be home in time for lunch."

****

The couple burrowed beneath a downey comforter in brisk darkness. Their breath and bodies entwined, too exhausted to sleep.

"Thank you for coming here," Zaira whispered.

"I'm honored you asked." Jacob kissed his wife's forehead. "Childhood summers with your aunt and uncle influenced who you are, my beautiful witch."

Zaira pressed her lips against her her husband's parted mouth. Their tongues met in the middle. She loved the way Jacob tasted, the way he smelled, the way his firm body fit against hers, adjoining pieces of the same perfect puzzle.

"Magic has hold of me." He pulled her closer.

"It takes two to cast a love spell," she murmured between kisses. "We are even."

****

Their relationship began with glances, eleven months earlier.

Zaira first observed Jacob in the university cafeteria, adjacent to the hospital. He was sometimes alone, sometimes with other scrubs-wearing students, looking handsome, smart and sleepy, always sipping black coffee, regardless of meal or time of day. Creatures of habit, she preferred a small grouping of tables in a peaceful corner away from the din of clanking trays and canned music, across the narrow walkway from his larger more lively choice spot. He didn't appear to be distracted by noise or commotion, only by her presence. Their lingering gazes progressed over weeks into shy smiles, nods, and the occasional *hello* if near one another in the salad queue or checking out at the cashier.

Zaira was the first to initiate *real* contact. She unclipped paper from her binder, penned a short note, and handed it to Jacob before heading to her graduate class, long way through the dining hall, out the aft double doors, not turning around to see if he was watching her purposeful procession. No need. She could feel his eyes fixed upon her.

He was staring, heart racing, palm making damp the folded loose leaf clutched in his grip. When Jacob was sure she was gone from view, he opened the page.

> ### *Should you get a break from cutting up cadavers,*
> ### *I spend quite a bit of time alone in the library stacks, 800's.*
> ### *Zaira*

It was a declaration as well as an invitation. Jacob slid the correspondence into his pocket and reread it over the next two days, devouring each word more times than he could acknowledge without blushing.

On the third day Jacob found himself with a free hour, a frayed note, and a quest to finally meet the blue-eyed brunette who'd invaded his waking and scant slumbering hours.

The main library elevator descended further than Jacob deemed possible, to a dimly lit subterranean abyss laden with volumes of musty literature. Zaira was waiting in the tiny foyer when the doors slid open.

"So glad. I knew it would be you." Her smile confirmed the statement. Zaira reached for Jacob's hand when he stepped off the lift. She laced her fingers between his, neither forward nor timid about making physical contact.

Jacob felt as if he'd been grounded. The immediate energy traveling between them, calm and gentle with a passionate pulse awakening.

Zaira spent the hour introducing him to her leather-bound companions, Shaw, Goldmith, Joyce, Beckett, Wilde, Yeats, Stoker, and the thesis mission they'd inspired.

Neither wanted the time to end. They promised with a kiss to meet again, as soon as possible. His schedule more demanding than hers, get togethers comprised of quick meals in the cafeteria, caresses in the stacks, cuddling upon a park bench. Eventually, encounters moved to her apartment, a third-floor studio walkup near campus. Jacob arrived at odd hours with no prior notice.

Zaira always eager for her lover's visit. She enjoyed having him in her bed, bath, smelling his body on her skin and sheets after he'd gone. They made love often, uninhibited, bestowing carnal pleasures neither had experienced before. Zaira relished taking Jacob to heaven in her mouth, tasting her own juices on him after he'd returned the gift with his tongue, lips, fingers.

Their bodies, brains always in sync, Jacob and Zaira acknowledged early on that they were meant to be together, always. Kindred spirits. The only pending hurdle between them discussed in detail was logistical, his out-of-town residency, her dissertation. She volunteered to commute. The fact that they came from different clans only once considered, on the morning Jacob proposed. "We both have enough of a break coming up to take a honeymoon," Jacob declared when Zaira opened her eyes from a post copulation slumber. "Think we can find a rabbi and priest to marry us tomorrow?"

"Doubt it." Zaira reached for a book in her nightstand and consulted a series of charts. "There's a new moon on Wednesday and Venus is direct. Couldn't ask for a better blessing from the Universe. I will marry you then.

On Wednesday they said secular "I do's" at City Hall. Zaira wearing a belted powder blue shift, Jacob in khakis, navy blazer, and borrowed tie that complimented his sea green eyes. They brought along matching department store rings and two witness friends. The quartet celebrated afterwards with an early dinner at their favorite sushi bar. Following the saki toast, Zaira and Jacob called their parents with the news.

Jacob's mother cried. A *shiksa* had stolen her son.

Zaira's parents preached the sinfulness of an unsanctified union and threatened to boycott any celebrations.

Their reactions didn't matter to the beaming newlyweds. Firestorms were a necessary part of the life cycle. When the smoke cleared and embers turned to fertile soil, a stronger forest always emerged. The parental predicament only required time to recover.

Since families were not part of the nuptials, Jacob and Zaira decided to make heritage a focus of their honeymoon. They would pay a visit to each other's roots. First stop Ireland, last stop Israel, a location neutral Roman holiday weekend in between.

****

"Your aunt and uncle are more liberal-minded than I expected." Jacob's tone conveyed relief.

"Aunt Bridget sips black current brandy all day long and judges no one except Uncle Cecil," Zaira replied. "My uncle would only mind if you were a descendant of Oliver Cromwell or a fan of Arsenal Football Club." She squeezed Jacob's hand, which was resting on her belly.

"Still, Ireland is a devout Catholic country," Jacob reminded.

"On the surface," Zaira remarked. "The same Irish Catholic you meet at mass on Sunday will treat a wart by rubbing it with snail slime, during a full moon. They'll then hang the creature by a string from a tree. As the moon wanes and the snail decays, so too will the wart disappear. Mother Nature's magic and pagan practices exist today. The Church decries it, but the Irish live and die by it. We're all witches."

****

The honeymooners awoke to the sound of Cecil's ancient diesel lorry backfiring and sputtering down the drive and along the gravel way leading to the main road.

Jacob reached over his wife and unfastened the window shutter, letting in a pre-dawn breeze. "G'morning. How many hours of creaky bed playtime do we have until they return?"

"Good morning, my love." Zaira slipped free of her nightgown while Jacob removed his briefs and t-shirt. "Four or five hours."

They made love hard and swift, like two athletes coaxing one another across the finish line in a draw. Morning's chill was not sufficient to keep rising writhing body heat at bay. Orgasmic gymnastics lasted until bright sun commandeered blue sky. Duvet discarded, pillows tossed, sheets damp with perspiration and spilled seed, the couple rested, Zaira's head on Jacob's chest.

"Wouldn't mind seeing that watering hole your aunt and uncle were arguing about last night." Jacob brushed a lock of hair away from his wife's flushed cheek.

"As you wish." Zaira nudged Jacob. "Better get moving if we want breakfast, lake visit, and another romp before Uncle Cecil and Aunt Bridget return. Pond Lough is about a twenty minute walk across the south pasture."

****

Pond Lough was nestled amid a clutch of oak trees that provided the herd shade on occasional hot afternoons, cover during more frequent rains. On this day the dairy cows and their calves were elsewhere, grazing in knee-high August grasses along the bluff.

Jacob surveyed the serene scene. "Not much of a lake, but definitely bigger than a pond." He tossed a stick into the water.

"Expecting Lady of the Lake to catch your Excaliber?" Zaira teased.

"If there was a Lady of the Lake, she would have perished by now, succumbed to a bacterial infection from agricultural e-coli." Jacob took a step back from the shore. "A hundred cows and a thousand years of rain washing manure down hill into this basin isn't a healthy combination."

"Well, Dr. Doom N. Gloom, King Arthur probably had bad teeth and bed bug bites on his privates, but it's not romantic to mention." Zaira removed her shoes and began to disrobe. "Filth and demons be damned, I'm going swimming."

"Please don't!" Before Jacob could plead again, Zaira ran naked into the water and dived beneath the surface.

Decades of fallen leaves and thriving weeds made visibility nonexistent. Zaira figured if she was going to prove or disprove Uncle Cecil's claim, she'd need to venture further out. With five big strokes she propelled herself to the lake's center.

"You're very brave," Jacob called from his *terra firma*. "How about returning to shore?"

"Clear past the initial muck." Zaira treaded water, her hands creating ripples along the surface. "Not as cold as I recall, either. Must be a hot spring feeding in somewhere. I'm going down, see if there's a bottom. Then I promise to swim back."

Body buoyancy made Zaira's descent slow. Five feet, ten feet, fifteen, she could tell approximately how deep by the amount of pressure building in her ears. Toes touched mud. She canvassed the area. Nothing unusual, black fish, fallen tree. Viewing rewards didn't warrant the angst Zaira knew Jacob was experiencing, waiting for her to reemerge. She exhaled. Bubbles effervescing through her nose made it difficult for Zaira to see what awaited above. Half way through the assent she brushed against a huge hard and hairy object. Red-eyed Holstein, still sporting her bell. Zaira swore Bessie lunged, teeth bared. The nude diver shot to the surface, didn't stop kicking until she reached shore.

Jacob led his trembling wife out of the slippery mire to the grassy bank and handed her her clothes. "What happened?"

"Uncle Cecil's cow is down there, Jacob. She tried to attack me."

Jacob didn't reply. No need; his visage displayed disbelief.

"You're thinking I have a vivid imagination, but I know what I saw." Zaira buttoned her checkered blouse.

"Very possible there's a dead cow down there," Jacob said. "Drowned animal became caught on something, which is why her carcass didn't float to the surface. Cold water slowed decomposition. Rotting flesh is..." He paused.

"Unhealthy and disgusting, I know, but Jacob, Bessie wasn't decayed and her eyes were red." Zaira took her husband's hand and led him back to the bank. "Please, see for yourself so you don't think I'm crazy."

"Just because I don't also dream about dearly departed relatives or hear spirit guide voices chattering in my head, doesn't mean I think you're crazy."

Jacob stopped short of getting his sneakers wet. "We both have our own unique abilities. Let's go back to the cottage. You need a shower."

"Scared?" Zaira had that coy *I dare you* expression on her face.

The *look* Jacob succumbed to on most occasions, like when Zaira's look coaxed him into making love standing upright against bookcases or sitting atop armless reading chairs in the library stacks, or the times Jacob forced himself to keep a straight face in a restaurant as she played footsies with his crotch. "Ok." He disrobed down to briefs. "Some body parts require protection." Jacob made a running start and plunged into the pond.

Zaira applauded. "I knew my Junior Olympian swimming campion husband would take a dive for me!"

To the center and down swam Jacob. He considered hovering a few feet below the surface before returning to shore and telling Zaira he hadn't encountered anything except fish. However, he didn't have a chance. There in front of him was the Holstein, just as Zaira had described. Red-eyed Bessie opened her mouth and aimed jaws. Without contemplation, Jacob propelled forward first, yanked the rope from around her neck, and made like Michael Phelps towards shore. "Zaira!" He waved the clanging cow bell between strokes. "Souvenir!"

"My hero!" Zaira cheered.

A split second later, Jacob made an abrupt disappearance beneath the water's surface. Bessie grabbed hold of his briefs and was fast dragging him down, down, down towards what appeared to be a cavern at the bottom of the lake. Jacob fought with fury to release his waistband from her toothy grip. Pressure in his ears building, the duo was deep. Jacob hadn't prepared his lungs for a dive. Need for air would soon be critical.

"Jacob!"

He heard his wife's faint muffled cry in the dark distance. Bessie had reached the cave opening. Jacob dropped her bell and grabbed hold of the limestone transom in time to prevent the beast from pulling him in. She tugged. He held tight, knees scraping against rock, her teeth a perilous distance from his torso. Jacob's lungs burned, vision began to blur.

The elastic around his waist stretched and tore. The demon cow released the flaccid fabric and lunged for Jacob's leg. He saw an opportunity and thrust a foot into the beast's snout. Like a startled shark she froze, then retreated. Jacob made for daylight.

Zaira met him at the surface and guided his bloodied battered body back to shore.

For a long while Jacob and Zaira recovered in each other's arms upon the green grass. No explanatory words uttered between them.

Jacob broke the silence. "Sorry."

"You're apologizing?" Zaira protested. "I'm the fool who goaded her husband into a haunted lake. I forced to you come face-to-face with—"

Jacob placed a silencing finger against her lips. "Not ready to attempt making sense of what happened down there." He stood and offered his wife a hand up. "Come on. Let's get showered. We could both use a *shluf* before lunch."

The damp divers made their way back to the cottage, arriving as their hosts exited the rusty little lorry parked in the drive.

"Aye, you've been swimming!" Aunt Bridged clutched a wicker basket filled with fresh produce and rustic breads covered in cloth. "Acquired an appetite, I'm sure. The noon meal's soon to be served."

Zaira whispered to Jacob. "So much for a shower, *shluf,* and romp." She kissed his cheek and addressed her aunt. "I'm happy to help with lunch while Jacob unloads feed and supplies with Uncle Cecil."

After aunt and niece entered the cottage, Uncle Cecil placed a confiding arm across Jacob's shoulder. "Well, lad, if ya don't believe a demon haunts me lough, how 'bout we go 'round back and I'll introduce ya to the leprechaun what lives beneath me shed…"

THE END

ELMER'S BLUFF

After deep nasal exploration and retrieval, Wayne examined his glutinous find with interest before flicking it onto an empty desk.

Maggie, having viewed the excavation and catapulting, turned several shades of pale before returning to her natural ruddy hue. She scribbled, *I hate Wayne! He's a gross booger picker!* on a torn sheet of notebook paper and tossed it to her best friend Annie in the back row.

Annie in turn drew a cartoon of the act and promptly lobbed the paper back.

With valuable space still remaining on the note, Maggie contemplated additional boredom-busting blather. Sister Mary Ignatius's wiry menopause mustache would do. Maggie couldn't help but giggle as she described her prim habit-wearing teacher dusting food bits off her top lip, or perhaps she had a holy grooming comb? Better yet, Sister might allow Wayne to pick the crumbs.

"Margaret O'Leary." Sister Mary Ignatius's shrill voice prompted Maggie's pen to dash across the page in a startled streak. "What are you doing?"

Not an instant to spare, Maggie pulled a plastic bottle from her pencil case, squeezed a liberal amount of Elmer's Glue onto the contraband correspondence, folded it in four, and with a single swift move had the loose leaf square concealed in the sleeve of her uniform sweater. When it came to making incriminating pen melt and vanish, Elmer's Glue was mother superior to White-Out.

"Standup and answer me," continued the Dominican inquisitor. "Miss O'Leary. What were you doing, instead of listening to my reading of <u>King Lear</u>?"

"Nothing."

"Nothing will come of nothing; speak again." Sister Mary Ignatius beamed. She delighted in any opportunity to recite Shakespeare, and an opportunity to recite in context from her current lesson was an exceptional treat. Sister allowed her satisfied silence to linger before continuing. She placed veiny hands upon bony hips. "Saw you working amusingly away at something. I am neither a fool nor am I blind. Now tell me, Miss O'Leary, before I make a notation on your behavior card, what were you doing?"

"I was writing," came the response.

"Writing what?"

"Nothing." Maggie locked her knees to keep them from becoming fondue.

Sister Mary Ignatius stepped out from behind her desk. "It is impossible to write *nothing*, Miss O'Leary."

Maggie corrected herself. "I wasn't writing anything." She immediately gathered from Sister's exasperated expression that that too was an unacceptable reply. Maggie's complexion flushed red to ruby. If that weren't enough embarrassment, at this moment of agonizing scrutiny, Maggie felt a sneeze approaching. She gasped, puckered, blinked, and rearranged her face in a successful effort to stifle it.

"Don't mock me with ridiculous expressions," Sister scolded, raising her voice an octave higher. "Come here and bring your notebook."

Maggie's heart thumped with the ferocity of a demon-possessed drum. She gathered her battered spiral under the glare of fifty feasting eyes. If not for Annie's pained grimace of moral support, Maggie would have felt completely betrayed.

Sister remove a yellow shiny unsharpened pencil from a never-used Vatican souvenir coffee cup, which sat upon an unblemished blotter, atop a clutter-free desk, that had beside it an empty plastic-lined trash receptacle. Even the air surrounding Sister smelled antiseptic. "Place your notebook on my desk, Miss O'Leary."

Maggie obeyed.

Sister Mary Ignatius flipped open its frayed cover with the eraser end of her inspection instrument. Pizza stained page one, in Sister's opinion, warranted two tongue clicks. Page two...Page three... Two additional tongue clicks... Page four...

The deliberate pace gnawed at Maggie's nerves.

Page five... "Numerous incomplete assignments, Miss O'Leary." Page six... Page seven... Sister Mary Ignatius stopped at page seven where Maggie had written in purple magic marker:

AMERICAN MORONS ROCK!
MAGGIE LOVES TREY GARBAGE
MAGGIE + TREY = 4 LIFE

"Class." Sister Mary Ignatius's saccharine voice employed. "Allow me to read what Miss O'Leary doodles while she should be recording lecture notes."

Maggie's blouse moistened. Her stomach lurched. She prayed that she would faint or vomit or perform some other feat that would silence her tormentor and necessitate an immediate trip to the nurse's office. Instead, Maggie strained to contain a torrent of tears that were rapidly blurring her vision.

Sister Mary Ignatius read page seven aloud twice more. "Miss O'Leary is in love with an American moron, class."

More than a few callous classmates found Maggie's plight amusing. Sister Mary Ignatius too let out a snicker.

Maggie sensed another sneeze approaching. Her eyes squinted as she gasped in a succession of short breaths.

"Ew! Germs!" Sister Mary Ignatius screeched, thrusting a fist-full of heavy-duty tissues at Maggie, while at the same time covering her own nose and mouth with a crisp white handkerchief. "Turn away from me!" She scooted out of spray range.

"Achoo!" Maggie deliberately exaggerated. "Achoo!" followed a second, more amplified sneeze. "Achoo!" the third bellicose sneeze shook Maggie's entire body and forced her folded gluey secret out of hiding.

"Miss O'Leary." Sister Mary Ignatius scowled. "What is that?"

"Nothing," came Maggie's feeble reply through a river of tears.

Sister Mary Ignatius appeared triumphant. "Well then, Miss O'Leary," her smooth sweet voice returned. "Pickup *nothing* and bring it to me."

Maggie pried the gluey paper square from the linoleum and placed it in Sister's extended palm. It stuck.

"Miss O'Leary! What the—?"

"I can explain." Maggie stammered. "You see, Wayne dug a booger out of his nose and flicked it onto the empty desk next to me."

Sister Mary Ignatius flinched and winced at the mention of flying snot.

Maggie realized her advantage—her mortification morphed into opportunity. She went for the kill. "And I cleaned it off with that paper."

"Booger!" Sister Mary Ignatius screamed, her arms and legs contorting in a futile effort to rid herself of the adhesive. "It's on me!"

"I didn't want anyone to catch a green mucus disease or ebola."

"Ebola!" the frenzied woman moaned. "Get me rubbing alcohol, in my desktop drawer!" Sister pleaded as she chased herself about like a wormy dog.

Instead of retrieving, Maggie opened the classroom door.

Out sped Sister, ricocheting down the hall, through double doors, toward the nurse's office. The pubescent voyeurs who'd scurried from their seats spied with delight as their teacher writhed out of sight.

As if to signal the spectacle's end, the commencement bell rang.

Annie handed Maggie her notebook and backpack. Together they hurried to secure seats next to one another, and far away from Wayne, on the homeward-bound bus.

THE END

BROKEN PROMISES

From his dais seat of honor Father Gabriel's faded sable eyes, shielded behind bifocals, scanned his well-wishers. They were gathered around foldable dining tables, clustered across the gymnasium floor. He recognized families and faces and recalled many and varied defining incidents he'd witnessed and heard confessed over five decades. When the octogenarian arrived at Our Lady of Sorrows there was a Catholic in the White House and Beatles on the charts. *Much has changed about the world*, he thought. *But little about men.*

The Jesuit vowed to himself at the commencement of his tenure: Every parishioner deserved respect and the assurance that no matter what happened in the secular realm, his church would always be a safe sanctuary. Father Gabriel's promises met with reality. He'd fostered favorites, turned a blind eye to papal sanctioned prejudices and omissions, and swallowed more than his fair share of the blood in futile effort to quiet carnal urges. Lifetime had proved Father Gabriel was wholly human.

The matron of ceremonies stood behind a green and gold crepe paper adorned podium and glanced at a note delivered by messenger student. "As you know, Senator Grasso, our most eminent congregation member, promised to preside over this evening's retirement event. Unfortunately, last minute, he was called to a fundraiser function." She slid the folded correspondence into her pantsuit pocket. "He will be detained a little longer." There were mumbles and grumbles from the audience. "Not to worry, this provides ample opportunity for our very talented choir to entertain us, once again."

The choir commenced a round of dirges, having earlier exhausted their more cheerful song repertoire.

Father Gabriel was lulled into a boredom trance. The memory scene before his glazed gaze came into focus...

****

An ancient housekeeper dressed in mourning black led Gabriel down the rectory entry hall to a stairway accessible through what appeared to have been a pantry or closet, remains of door hinges marred the archway frame.

"Not a forever," assured the housekeeper, her accent thick, Italian, although Gabriel would later learn she'd been in America since the age of nine. "When Father Thomas go, you move a his room." She pointed right. "Nice a, with big a window."

Gabriel thanked his escort and made way up the narrow assent, shoulders scrunched, valise in front of him like a masthead. He was relieved to find his temporary quarters offered more space than anticipated, party due to sparse furnishings. Against the wall was a twin bed covered in starched sheets, a knitted blanket folded at the foot and sham-covered pillow at the head. Beside the bed was a small single-drawer nightstand that held a shaded lamp and wind-up clock, correct time set. On the other side of the eight-by-ten room was an open wardrobe that contained three wire hangers. Beside it was a wooden chair, bath towel and wash rag draped across the seat, paper-wrapped bar of Lux soap atop. On the windowless back wall hung a metal crucifix, tied to it a dried frayed strip of palm.

Gabriel set case upon bed and removed his few belongings, the last of which was a tarnished silver locket threaded through a broken chain. He opened the clasp to reveal a tiny black & white photo inside—himself ten years earlier, standing beside Sarah. Gabriel believed her to be the most beautiful woman ever to grace God's Earth.

It was summer. They were tanned, smiling, dressed in picnic attire, Sarah's long untamed ginger hair loosely pulled away from her freckled face with a white headband, her shoulder against Gabriel's arm. In the section of photo trimmed over a half century earlier, their fingers also touched, sealing the promise Gabriel made to Sarah, minutes before— they would become engaged as soon as he finished college. In the meantime, the locket would be a reminder of their future together.

God had other plans.

Sarah did not accept the news of Gabriel's calling as piously as he had hoped. When he drove five hours home from school one winter weekend with "something important" to tell, Sarah was sure "something important" would include a diamond ring.

"A priest?" Gabriel could clearly recall Sarah's incredulous questioning. "Give me up? Give up children? For a life of poverty and celibacy? Is this a joke? Are you ill?"

"I have never been more clear-minded or at peace," Gabriel replied. "I love God, even more than I love you."

"So much for promises." Sarah yanked the locket and chain from around her neck and handed them to Gabriel. "May you and your God live happily ever after."

There was a knock at the door.

Gabriel concealed the locket in his closed palm. "Come in."

Father Thomas entered. He was a height-deprived portly man. Made Gabriel think of Pooh and the honey tree, and he nearly wondered aloud how Father Thomas hadn't gotten lodged between the walls on his way up.

"Welcome to Our Lady of Sorrows," the priest said, brogue, scent of tobacco, and whiskey tinging his words. "Do me a favor, now? Take tonight's confessions? It's me duty Friday, but I'm not feeling me self this evening. Fresh air would do a bit a good, and the Red Sox are home against the Yankees. Monsignor has six box tickets for the house. He didn't expected you'd arrive 'til tomorrow."

"Sure." Gabriel smiled. "I'm a Dodgers fan, anyway."

****

"Father, wake up." the pantsuited emcee whispered. Her voice conveyed panic. "The choir is about to finish, Senator Grasso still hasn't arrived, and the kitchen isn't ready to serve. Everyone looks weary. What should I do?"

"These people have been patient long enough." Father Gabriel took it upon himself to fill the remaining time before dinner. He walked to the podium, recent remembrances on the forefront of his mind. "I recall the first confession I heard at Our Lady of Sorrows, fifty years ago. The worst. It worried me what sort of parish I'd come to."

Priests promise confessional confidentiality. The private topic of soul-bearing awoke most of the audience.

"A young fellow bragged that he'd stolen his neighbor's car, taken it for a joy ride, then lied to the police when questioned, successfully blaming the theft on a black man, who then did time in jail for the crime he did not commit."

There were audible gasps from the parishioners.

"He also said that he'd swindled money from his parents and from his employer, but he didn't stop there." Father Gabriel lowered his head. "The fellow also found it funny that he'd forced himself on his fiancé's mother when he drove her home on the night of the engagement party, after spiking the poor woman's punch with sleeping tablets to the point where she had become incapacitated."

By this time the crowd was fully awake and attentive.

"You can imagine my thoughts…" Father Gabriel allowed a purposeful pause. "However, I'm pleased to say, as the weeks passed I realized that this sad excuse for a Catholic and a human being was the exception. Our Lady of Sorrows parish proved to be a place of kind decent people."

At this moment Senator Grasso arrived ceremoniously, his dark-suited, walkie-talkie-carrying entourage bounding through the gymnasium's swinging double doors, clearing a path for their boss. He apologized for being late and was keen to commandeer the podium— an election year and room filled to capacity with a captive voting audience.

Father Gabriel returned to his seat.

Senator Grasso bellied up to the microphone and removed a prepared speech from his breast pocket. "Half-century may seem like an eternity, but I personally will always remember the day Father Gabriel came to Our Lady of Sorrows," the life-long politician read. "In fact, I was the first parishioner he heard in confession."

THE END

FEARS OF A CLOWN

"Coulrophobia," Elizabeth read aloud before tearing the diagnosis from its binding. She returned the defaced psychology tome to its bookshelf, settled into a worn leather sofa, and then slid the pilfered page between World History and French II hardcover texts in her schoolbook satchel.

It was three o'clock. The antique cuckoo chimed. Dr. Weiss entered. He was an affable man in his sixties, above average height, with a full head of coarse hair, more pepper than salt. He walked with a pronounced limp, and had an odd-shaped tattooed left arm that reminded Elizabeth of an opened paperclip.

"Good afternoon, Miss Collins," Dr. Weiss greeted his young patient, an element of Eastern European motherland evident in his cadence. He seated himself behind a cluttered Victorian-era desk. "As I recall…" The pediatric psychiatrist sifted through a stack of yellow writing tablets. "Ah, here it is." He reviewed a page that began with a short descriptive analysis: *highly intelligent/ precocious/ difficulties with right and wrong.* "According to my notes you were about to share recollections when our last session ended. You believe there's a direct correlation between Aunt Philippa—"

"And my night terrors, yes," Elizabeth interjected.

"Tell me what you recall."

"May I read, instead?" Elizabeth removed a journal from her purse. "I'm going to be a famous author one day, so I've written my memories into a story, of sorts."

"Very well, begin." Dr. Weiss smiled and leaned back in his chair.

****

School ended and we relocated to our lakeside country retreat near Creighton.

I remember it was one of those summer mornings that calls out to be reveled in from the first glimmer of daylight. My little brother Henry and I were poised to respond when Mother intercepted. Much to our annoyance we had to bathe, dress in our best, and sit on the porch with strict orders not to stray. Even Churchill, our Great Pyrenees dog, was washed and locked in the kitchen to dry for what was turning into an *occasion.*

"Your Auntie Philippa will be arriving shortly, after a long family absence," Mother explained. "My elder sister will be staying with us until she is re-acclimated, finds suitable employment, and a place of her own to rent."

"Oh, why?" Henry protested. "Father says she's a nutter who used to live in a broken bus with bald people who say they are invisible."

"Henry!" Mother scolded.

"If she's bald and invisible, how are you certain she's your sister?" I asked.

"Her hair has grown a bit and she is completely visible." Mother exhaled and folded her arms, which is her way of saying the conversation has ended. Don't know why Father and Henry haven't figured that out yet, would save them a world of grief.

Case in point, my brother lost two days of cartoons when he removed his clip-on tie and launched himself backwards onto the glider in continued protest, screaming, "Who cares? This shirt is choking me and we never even met Auntie Philippa before!"

Or so he mistakenly thought.

Around nine, a blue van pulled into the drive beside our cottage. Two stern-looking uniformed men carrying pointy poles stepped out of the vehicle's driving compartment. One stood sentry while the other opened the van's wide slid door. All the passengers inside began making bird noises and tried to exit at once. The sentry used his stick to poke them back into their seats while Auntie gathered her bags. After she walked to the porch, the driver asked Mother to sign a clipboard form and then the two men jumped back into the van and sped away, as if their arrival were a game of tag, and Mother was now *it.*

Before hellos were exchanged, Auntie Pippa, as she preferred to be called, tried to coax our memories with a bizarre narrative about giving Henry and me our first spankings. We were toddlers at the time, and she watched us while Mother and Father were at a function.

"Spanking babies?" If Henry had any hidden interest in liking or welcoming Auntie Pippa, it vanished at that instant. My brother's jaw and fists were clenched and he appeared ready and able to successfully defend our younger selves.

Mother stepped in between her son and her sister.

Auntie Pippa seemed unawares that she had narrowly escaped retribution. "Physical touch of all sorts conditions the body to withstand the rigors of life," Auntie explained, her eyes glazed, voice sweet and sing-song. A gypsy scarf partially covering her peach fuzz head jingled as she made sweeping gestures towards the sky. "Spanking awakens our memory of oneness with universal energies, the vail separating consciousness and dimensions."

"Father was correct," I said. "Henry, we better go find a poking stick."

Mother gave me *the look*, so instead I carried Auntie's bags, paper grocery totes, to her room, which was in fact my room that I'd been instructed to share. At least I could keep the top bed bunk. Churchill was still in the kitchen, not yet informed that he had been evicted from the bottom bed bunk.

Auntie Pippa asked me to remain while she unpacked and put her belongings into an emptied drawer in my dresser. I obliged, out of curiosity. Her wardrobe consisted of three gypsy scarves folded inside sandwich plastic, three dark gray striped dresses, identical to the one she was wearing, and three pair of light gray bloomers with the words **Property Of** printed on the rear. Besides clothing, she had one bag that contained polished stones in various colors, two crystal necklaces, and a disassembled blender. Auntie put on a neckless. The clear four-inch stalactite hung long atop her dress, between her braless breasts, which also hung. In fact, every bit of chalky white skin on Auntie Pippa's thin frame hung. She reminded me of a balloon that had been repeatedly filled to capacity, then deflated.

"This sacred crystal repels demons and cleanses auras." Auntie reached towards me.

Before I realized her intent, it was too late. Auntie's arms had clenched me like a vise.

"Protection may also be transferred through hugging," she said. "Tighter the better." Skinny but strong, Auntie Pippa knocked the wind out of me. I had only enough.

breath remaining for a weak whimper distress call. Too low for my brother to hear, but loud enough to send Churchill bounding from the kitchen, to the rescue.

"Dog!" Auntie released me at the sight of him. "I am deathly allergic to dogs!" She leapt onto my top bunk, as remarkably nimble as a cat. Her flight and accompanying flails and shrieks prompted Churchill into a jumping-wagging-barking frenzy that summoned Mother and Henry.

"What is going on here?" Mother demanded.

"Auntie tried to squeeze me to death," I said. At that moment the event clues came together. "She's a mutant boa constrictor. That's why Auntie Pippa's skin is saggy and her eyes are foggy. She is about to shed."

Auntie's shrieks became gasps and coughs. A raised red patch appeared on her face.

"Pippa, what is the matter?" Mother looked as concerned as she was annoyed. She touched her sister's cheek. "Are you taking medications? Where are they?"

"Top drawer. Dog," Auntie wheezed. "Allergic."

"Henry, put Churchill outside. Elizabeth, fetch a glass of water and a damp cloth," Mother directed, after examining the label on a bottle of Auntie's pills. "Pippa, I do not recall you having a dog allergy. Our father raised hunting hounds."

When her medicine had been ingested and rash subsided, Auntie Pippa told Mother about some of her other new fears and ailments. Besides dogs, she could not be exposed to hat pins, strollers, mix-matched socks, kites other than the traditional four-point shape, dripless candles, empty coffee cans, organ music, belly lint, soiled toilet tissue, crayon shavings, and holiday-themed sweaters. An assortment of allergies and aversions were not the only conditions to plague Auntie Pippa. She had also forgotten how to chew. All meals and snacks were required to be mashed in the blender (water added when necessary) and served with a spoon or straw.

"Who forgets how to chew?" Henry asked. "Bet if we stuck a good gob of warm taffy into Auntie's mouth she'd remember."

Mother threatened severe punishment if we attempted to prove Henry's theory.

Our summer was off to a miserable start, that worsened.

Churchill was banished to the garden and howled in sorrow every night. Father made unconvincing work excuses so as not to drive up from the city to visit on weekends, and in less than a month's time, Mother changed from cheery to weary. Only Auntie was thriving. And why not? Everyone and everything revolved around her *issues*, as Mother called them.

Henry and I did our utmost to misbehave in hopes of summoning one of the demons Auntie Pippa so often talked about warding away. It was our plan to destroy the sacred crystals and pay handsomely from our allowances if the demons would drag Auntie back to Hell and keep her there, at least until school began and we returned home. Unfortunately, no demons appeared, and our strategy only made Mother more haggard, and earned Henry and me additional protective hugs from Auntie.

We had run out of problem-solving ideas. Our lone place of solace became the lake.

Henry and I had taken our rafts out one afternoon and were enjoying a restful paddle when we heard an all too familiar voice arrive on the wind. "Hen-ry! E-liz-a-beth!" I thought Auntie's call must be coming from a nightmare I'd lulled into, but Henry heard it too. We looked-up and there on the shore stood saggy Auntie Pippa, dressed in her **Property Of** bloomers with a gypsy scarf fashioned into an ill-fitted halter top. No visible crystal, but she was holding a broken black umbrella and waving it at us.

"Mother must have lied down for a nap," I surmised. "Ignore Auntie, Henry, and she will eventually leave."

It was impossible, however, to follow my own directive when a lifeguard tentatively approached Auntie Pippa and said something while pointing towards of the ladies' changing cabin. Auntie recoiled. The lifeguard stepped closer and took hold of her forearm. It was the wrong move. Auntie let out a cry that sent sunbathers scurrying from their blankets. "You are not taking me away! I am a free citizen of this universe and have the right to remain in my realm!" She opened and closed the misshapen umbrella like a bellows. "Stay back!"

"Won't be a boring day, after all!" Henry exclaimed. "And if crazy Auntie sees that stroller over there, it'll even be more exciting."

I spotted Mother's car in the parking area. She was already making her way in haste across the sand towards her sister's commotion. Auntie Pippa ceased her antics as soon as she too caught sight of Mother.

"Mother will make it all right and take Auntie Pippa home," Henry predicted correctly. He swung his raft half way around, in the direction of the boat pier. "Let's race to the other side!"

When we arrived back at the cottage, hungry and tired, a few hours later, Auntie was nowhere in sight and Mother was packing.

"May we run away too?" Henry asked.

"I am not exactly running away," Mother said. "However, I do have a large favor to ask of you and your sister. I am driving down to the city to see Father and attend a dinner tonight. I will be back first thing tomorrow morning. There's cold macaroni salad for supper in the fridge."

I attempted to speak.

"Let me finish, Elizabeth." Mother zipped her valise. "All I ask is that you two remain indoors, and out of trouble. In exchange for allowing me a much needed break, I will take you here." She handed Henry a flyer. "This was in our mailbox today."

"The circus!"

"Rides, cotton candy, clowns, elephants, dancing monkeys, aerialists, an arcade," I read over Henry's shoulder. "Opens Sunday."

"Promise?" My brother grinned and hugged the paper.

"Promise."

"Is it legal to leave an eleven and a thirteen year old alone with a mad woman?" I inquired, knowing full well I wouldn't be turning thirteen until September.

"No idea. Your father is the lawyer," Mother remarked. "What I do know is I have given Pippa enough medication to make her sleep until my return." She removed her car keys from their hook. "While I am gone, Churchill is permitted indoors."

Henry, Churchill, and I watched as Mother sped down the drive, almost as fast as the men in the blue van had after delivering Auntie.

We three were seated together on the sofa, eating macaroni and watching *The Adventures of Pirate Pete* when Auntie entered the parlor. She looked ridiculous, still dressed in her fake bathing clothes.

Churchill barked. Henry pulled him closer. "You are not supposed to wake up."

"Thought Mother gave you enough medicine to sleep for a long time?" I said.

"Held the pills under my tongue and then spit them when my sister left the room," Auntie confessed. "I don't want to sleep. I prefer to watch television." She eyed the sofa. "My back is in spasms. You three, sit on the floor. I must lie down."

"Oh, no," Henry replied. "We were here first. Go back to bed if you want to lie down."

Besides all of her other *issues*, Auntie Pippa was manipulative when it came to seating arrangements. If someone else was on the sofa or in the big soft dining room armed chair, Auntie would cry and claim that she had severe back pain, and force the seated person to give up their comfortable spot.

"Henry, I suspect Auntie's not half as ill as she pretends to be," I remarked, as if she wasn't present. "Churchill is five feet away and Auntie Pippa is not even coughing or covered in rashes."

"I am developing an immunity to this particular dog," Auntie explained. "Curing myself by adding his dander to blender meals and ingesting vitamins and amino antibodies."

"I don't understand what that means," replied Henry, who had begun yanking clumps of loose fur off Churchill and tossing it around the sofa like a protective amulet. "But I know malarkey when I hear it."

"Me too," I added. "We are excellent fib detectives."

Could tell Auntie Pippa believed herself bested and was deciding her next move. She wandered around the parlor until she came upon the circus flier. She shrieked.

"Oh, what now?" Henry moaned.

"I cannot be anywhere near a circus or carnival. I am terrified of clowns."

"Even clowns are afraid of clowns," Henry said. "Haven't you seen them always running away from one another?"

"True," I agreed. "And it isn't as if we invited you to the circus, anyway. No reason to spoil a perfectly pleasant outing. Now leave the room. We are trying to watch our show."

Auntie left the parlor, went into the adjacent kitchen, and turned on the blender. Besides the annoying noise, the machine caused our television to make a *shhhh* sound and go grey with squiggly static. After ten minutes of continued interruption, I sneaked across the floor to spy. What was she blending? I wasn't surprised to see the machine empty. It was all a ploy to steal the sofa.

"Auntie can't be allowed to ruin everything!" Henry yelled. The hum of the blender drowning his words.

It was the last straw.

Henry, Churchill, and I decided to retaliate, for everything. For Auntie making us miss our favorite television show, for her lying about dog allergies and causing Churchill to sleep in the garden all summer, and most of all for Auntie Pippa spanking us when we were toddlers.

We devised a plan…

****

"Let's turn off the television, Henry," I said loudly enough for Auntie to hear above the noise of her dumb blender that was starting to give off a burnt rubber smell. "How about we go outside on the porch and play a game?"

No sooner was the television off and Henry, Churchill, and I outside then Auntie was stretched out on the sofa watching a movie that had organ music and men and ladies kissing.

We sneaked off the porch and ran around back of the cottage, to our parent's bedroom window, which was open and easy enough for us to climb through. Once inside I went about painting Henry's face like a clown with Mother's red lipstick and white powders. I rummaged through her and Father's closets and found suitable clown attire: baggy pants, puffy blouse, and an old red floppy hat Father wore when he barbecued. When Henry was ready, I face-painted Mother's foam wig head and impaled it upon one of Father's golf clubs for my brother to carry, a second clown, creepy bald and hat-wearing.

"A poking stick!" remarked Henry.

We scurried back out the window and returned to the porch. As suspected, Auntie Pippa remained prone on the sofa, watching her movie.

I unscrewed the overhead fixture lightbulb, banged on the screen door, and cried, "Help! Help! He's after us!"

Auntie left the sofa and lowered the television volume. "What is going on out there?"

"Hurry, Auntie Pippa!" I pleaded in my actress voice as I hurried off the porch.

Auntie peeked outside. "Elizabeth?" All was dark and quiet. She opened the door and took a step, hesitated, then ventured a little further, step-by-step, into the garden moonlight until she came face-to-face with Henry the clown and his clown friend on a golf club.

We expected Auntie to shriek, but instead she took off running down the drive. Caught Henry and Churchill off-guard, but they fast recovered and pursued.

I went back into the cottage, changed the television channel, and waited on the sofa.

Henry and Churchill returned a half-hour later, perspired, tired, and victorious. "Guess she really is afraid of clowns. We chased Auntie past the lake, to the road that leads into town." Henry panted between sips of lemonade. "I poked her with the stick all the way."

Auntie Pippa did not return that night, or any other.

Seven months have passed. The police found no trace of Auntie and she has not contacted Mother with information regarding her whereabouts.

Henry is certain the demons found Auntie Pippa running along the road without her protective crystal. They dragged her back to Hell, where she rightfully remains.

Without proof, however, we are unable to verify my brother's theory.

"There you have it, Dr. Weiss." Elizabeth closed her journal. "Every night since last summer's events I wake up in terror, afraid that Auntie Pippa's disappearance was only a pleasant dream.

THE END

IN DEED

Indeed, neither in prayer nor in study could Chaim the boy remain reverent, pensive, motionless. His peaceful yet curious eyes were always fixed elsewhere, searching beyond the window, across the meadow and pond to the vast forest beyond. As the boy gazed, flora and fauna would summon him in nature's tongues, to run, to come, to learn of God not taught in books, by rote. The beckoning would eventually persuade Chaim, and when his teacher's back was turned he would hasten like a swift sudden gust of wind, through the door, across the green, towards his preferred classroom amid the trees.

Chaim's *rav* was vigorous and faster on his feet than the ten-year-old boy whom he would pursue and return to schooling.

A day arrived when Chaim answered Gideon's trumpeting swans in the sky above, but now instead of chase, the bested teacher called after his pupil, "Go, fly, deliver yourself, child. In deed, I have learned my lesson, not to interfere with the wild sages that summon you elsewhere from beyond."

Chaim became a companion of nature. He removed his tunic and dwelt with the beasts, slept in lairs and dens, at times with gentle rabbit, at others with observant fox. The boy ate seeds and berries, drank from clear cool brooks alongside deer and bear, and observed night's sky with wise owl upon high bough. He learned the wiles and ways of the creatures without creeds, only innate deeds through which to honor their essence and Maker. The boy became to understand in his soul Jewish law prohibiting *tza'ar ba'alei chayim*, the suffering of living creatures.

Each sunrise Chaim sang his prayers to the rhythm of morning's hushed symphony. Sometimes he would hear God's reply: words and thoughts, images and ideas. Revelations that filled Chaim's head, not from his ears, but rather through his heart.

The day came on Chaim's thirteenth birthday when it was time for the young man to return to his human teachers and follow their path.

Rebbe Chaim, as he grew to be, was a renowned and respected resident teacher of the roads, observing *shabbat*, celebrating holy days, and making sojourns in towns and villages, near and far, wherever and whenever the wind instructed him to go. Invitations of transport he always graciously declined. Rebbe Chaim walked, more often with company than alone.

One day a foreign merchant with laden ox ventured on foot off road to gather a switch with which to strike his paused porter. When the merchant returned he found Rebbe Chaim attending to the beast.

"A jagged stone lodged between heel and buttress." Rebbe Chaim removed the animal's source of discomfort and handed it to the traveler. He then took a sack from the burdened ox and placed it on his own back. "There is no need for rod."

The merchant dropped his willow branch and walked in silence beside the relieved ox and Rebbe Chaim, who was greeted oft by locals and pilgrims alike. The merchant listened and observed and finally spoke. "You are well known and well traveled. May I make an inquiry?"

"Indeed," the rebbe replied.

"I am journeying from Vilnius to the village in the valley and I am wondering if you know what I should expect of the people and sentiments there?"

"Tell me," Rebbe Chaim said. "How was your stay in Vilnius?"

"Horrid," the merchant remarked. "I am pleased to be away from the crowds and stench of that vile city. I found the people most rude and unwelcoming. When I first arrived I was greeted coldly with suspicion. *Schlock* the women yelled when I tried to sell them goods. My prices and practices were always in question and I was not made by the elders to feel a part of the merchant community, *mavens* all. City-dwellers keep to themselves and do not take kindly to strangers. So I wish to know, what should I expect of the village in the valley."

"I regret to inform you," the rebbe replied, "Your experience in the valley will be no different than it was in Vilnius."

"As I feared." The merchant spat. "Curse them. In deed people are the same."

Summer's mid-day sun was high and the road dusty and dry. Rebbe Chaim directed the merchant's attention to a rushing stream in the near distance. "Let us rest and quench our thirst."

"Time is money," the merchant responded. He took the sack from Rebbe Chaim and placed it and himself again upon the ox. "I must make my leave."

Rebbe Chaim bid him *shalom* and ventured to the water bank where he prayed thanks for the refreshing respite.

A short while later another merchant arrived at the stream. Before satisfying his own parched need he unburdened his donkey and led her to the shallows where she drank and rolled in the damp grass. Her contentment appeared to amuse the merchant who by then reclined beside the jenny and sipped from a leather flask he had filled with water.

"*Shalom.* I am going to the village in the valley," the second traveller called, upon seeing Rebbe Chaim who was also resting nearby. "Do you know what it is like there?"

"I do," the rebbe said. "But first tell me—from where do you journey?"

"The markets of Vilnius," the second merchant replied.

"How was that?" the rebbe asked.

"The city was a delight and wonder, exceeding my best expectations! I would have remained longer had I not committed to sell in the valley. From the moment of arrival in Vilnius I was made to feel a member of a large family. Elder merchants gave me much advice. Children ran to my dear jenny and fed her sweets from their hands. With me their parents were kind and generous as well, never *hondl* over price or *kvetsh* about the quality of my goods. I am saddened to have left there. Vilnius will always hold for me fond memories." The second merchant again inquired. "So what of the village in the valley?"

"The same as in Vilnius awaits." Rebbe Chaim smiled. "A blessed and hospitable place for you too, indeed."

THE END

DAY AT THE GAMES

A mob outside the iron gates let out a frenzied roar.

The ensuing energy palpable. Epeius trembled, closed his eyes, and shielded his face beneath covered calloused palms. *This must be a hallucination, a nightmare.* Epeius tried to convince himself he would soon awaken. Mica, his beautiful wife, would be reclining beside him, her gentle smile sympathetic. He would tell her of his horrible dream. Mica's kisses would comfort him, calm his thoughts, and they would laugh about it together over a meal of sweet bread and wine.

"Wake up, Greek!" A soldier prodded on the free side of the cage.

Epeius startled, sweat beaded across his forehead, reveries returned to reality. He breathed with purpose in attempt to control the irregular pounding of his heart and terror that twisted the sick pit of his stomach.

The Roman soldier appeared amused by the captive's angst. "Champions die too. You will soon have eternity to sleep," the armed sentry mocked before continuing patrol along the cage-filled corridor, his leather sandals making a scratching sound against the stone floor.

Epeius redirected his regard from the bars that confined him to the thongs of rawhide over woolen glove that covered his massive hands. The Romans called it *caestus*. He fingered the metal pieces sewn into the fringe shielding his knuckles, bits of iron that he'd employed to shatter men's heads and pulverize their brains. Epeius shut his eyes hard, driving graphic game images from his mind. In an instant he was again gone from this prison, walking among his flock in Macedonia. Mica was there in the dessert too, playing her music beside the lotus flowers, untamed fiery hair framing her face. In his dreams and fantasies she was always present. Without Mica there was no hope. Epeius was a man of large stature who once shunned aggression. Like the sheep he tended, he had been a peaceful shepherd. The soldiers came, took him away, forced him to war against the Romans. Captured by the enemy, Epeius was spared because of his size, and instead sentenced to the arena. A fate that dangled death before him daily, a gladiator no more fortunate than the lions, entertainment slaughter.

Epeius cursed his innate drive to survive.

The cries of the crowd above summoned his attention. Epeius squinted through a crack in his cage wall and observed the arena event. A *retiarius*, opposing a *secutor*, had him trapped within a net. At the urging of the mad masses, the *retiarius* ran the bound disarmed *secutor* through with his trident. The approval applause was immediate and deafening.

"Barbarians, monsters!" Epeius shouted. "I pray the gods send me a Roman for my next opponent!" From experience, Epeius knew what was about to occur. He respectfully lowered his head.

In the center of the arena was a small door called the *Porta Libitinensis*, an access through which bodies of the dead, critically wounded, and those unfit for fight would be dragged by hook to be fed to the wild animals. The most direct view of the exiting carnage was reserved for the magistrates and officials who had their stools placed along the front row, center stage.

Lounging in the location of honor this day was Cassius Regulus, corpulent self-appointed premier promoter of gladiator games in Pompeii. Seated beside him was his guest, Marcellus Claudius Marcus, Rome's commander of the eastern army. To the right of the general was his jet mountain of battle-scarred servant guard, called Benomar.

"Cassius, your contests bore me." Marcellus yawned.

"How can you criticize when I have assembled the greatest gladiators in the empire for your pleasure?" Cassius defended.

Marcellus spat a sip of wine onto his host's sandal. "Frauds and cowards! Your games are a lie!"

Cassius sprung from his seat.

Benomar did likewise.

Since he had been expelled from the Senate in Rome due to conduct unsavory for even a politician, Cassius had resurrected his reputation as a games promoter, his wish to one day return to Rome vindicated, to be appointed editor of the Circus Maximus. In response to his guest's stinging criticism, Cassius declared with pride, in a voice loud enough for surrounding spectators to hear above the din, "It is you who are a liar, Marcellus! I would match my gladiators against anyone, including your Benomar!"

A chilled hush permeated the box. Cassius paled. What insanity had prompted him to challenge the commander's guard? In front of a blood-thirsty crowd?

Marcellus Claudius Marcus stood with a waver, his balance compromised by wine, and the rising rage it fueled. Although not as tall or muscular as his servant, the commander's presence was equally intimidating. "Summon your best gladiator and we shall see who is a liar." The general's cadence was cold and calculated. "Your dubious honor and ten thousand *dinarlii* are at stake. I proclaim that Benomar will annihilate whomever is chosen."

The black giant nodded in agreement with his master.

A group of magistrates and officials of esteemed posts, evident by the purple borders on their togas, whispered and pointed; all eyes were upon Cassius.

A trickle of urine escaped Cassius's tunic and diluted the spat of wine pooled atop his sandal. The portly promoter knew he was in peril, as much from his own foolishness as Marcellus's drunken anger. "I accept your wager," Cassius replied, with all the scant conviction he could muster.

"Very well," Marcellus said. "Besides breastplate and shield, what weapons do you choose for your so-called gladiator?"

"Spear and short sword, for close fighting." Cassius doubted his hasty selection.

Both Marcellus and Benomar fell into a fit of laughter.

Cassius hurried out of the box to find a gladiator capable salvaging this debacle.

****

"I think I have the man you seek." Titus grinned, enjoying to no small degree the dependence Cassius had on his recommendation.

"Think? Think! I did not appoint you to think, Titus! I insist that you KNOW which of your men can prevail!" Cassius screamed. "If I lose my honor and my fortune, you will lose your life! Show him to me!"

Titus obeyed, led his employer down a steep ramp, around a dark fetid corridor lined with human coops that encompassed the interior perimeter of the arena.

Cassius soon found himself out of breath. "How much further?"

Titus increased his pace. For a man of sixty, he was a physical marvel. Titus had been a famous gladiator, besting every man and beast encountered, two hundred combats in all. Now he instructed gladiators. Cassius would have no game success without him.

"This is the man," Titus announced, stopping in front of the Greek's pen. "Epeius was a shepherd who became a hero soldier among the Macedonians. I have not trained a gladiator with more natural skill and resolve, nor have I encountered a man, besides myself, whose steadfast will to live channels fear into victory." Titus removed a key from his sash and unlocked the cage door. "Speak with him, if you wish."

Cassius borrowed Titus's sword and stepped into the cell.

Epeius retreated backwards until his taut broad back was against the aft enclosure wall. He struck a defensive pose.

Cassius halted and studied the prisoner before him. Epeius was in his early thirties, nearly as tall and broad as Benomar. What set them apart were the eyes. Where Benomar's displayed cruel confidence, Epeius's shone a far-away trance-like determination. "Impressive physique, but is he lucid?"

"As lucid as a trapped tiger that recalls its jungle home and yearns to return to it," Titus replied.

"What choice do I have? He will suffice," the promoter said. "Offer this Greek what we discussed and have him prepare for the next match." Cassius exited the cage. "I must return to my box. The stench sickens me. Send a messenger when ready."

Alone, Titus approached his gladiator. "This day will grant your freedom, either through death or victory," he said. "If by death, I will see to it that your remains receive proper burial. You have my word that hungry beasts will not feast upon your fallen flesh." Titus removed a purse from beneath his tunic. "If by victory, you will require these." He handed the purse to Epeius.

The gladiator unfastened the tie and removed a handful of silver, Caesar's profile adorned each coin.

"Affix the purse to the belt beneath your breastplate. No time to retrieve them if you win. Hasten from the arena to the end of this passage. The gate will be unlocked, and a chariot waiting to carry you to the port where a merchant ship sails tonight. Give the captain these coins and my word. You will be provided safe voyage home."

****

Silence hovered like a storm cloud above the stadium as the two titans stood twenty yards apart, spears raised, facing the box of honor where Cassius and Marcellus sat. The competitors awaited a sign to commence their contest.

Cassius lifted his arm, then let it fall.

At the same instant the opponents turned towards each other. Epeius peered past Benomar's shoulders, his eyes wide, weapon hands visibly trembling.

It was clear to the ebony warrior that his opponent was on the verge of panic. Benomar flashed a tooth-bared grin and circled, taunting Epeius with spear jabs and short sword thrusts, commencing what appeared to be a mismatched game of cat and mouse.

"A scared rodent, looking for a hole to hide." Marcellus leaned over the railing and laughed. "Tell me again, Cassius, your promised reward? To procure this coward as your servant guard should he be triumphant?"

Cassius did not reply.

Epeius tried to rid himself of the terror, the wave of dark despair that shook his body and commandeered his mind. Why would the promoter grant freedom when victory would increase his game value tenfold? No matter what Titus had promised, Epeius believed himself doomed, death his only escape.

Benomar charged, sword arm raised high.

Epeius reacted without thought. Lowering his spear and using the tip to catch hold of Benomar's sandal, off-balancing the giant and forcing him backwards in an awkward flailing effort to regain footing.

There was a collective gasp throughout the arena followed by a thundering chant: Epeius! Epeius! Epeius!

The Greek lifted his gaze to the last rows of the amphitheater. Standing on their feet were soldiers from Marcellus's own army, coaxing him on, extending a comradeship that only former adversaries could comprehend. A floating lithe figure appeared above the military crowd. Mica. She was cheering for him too. Epeius! Epeius! Epeius!

Benomar seethed. He lifted his spear and fired it with bullish strength.

Epeius stopped the projectile's flight with his shield, but the force of the blow staggered him, knocked his shield from his hands and him to the ground.

Delight displayed on Benomar's face. He rushed the fallen Greek.

Leather sandal upon slippery sand, Epeius struggled to stand. With no other defense option, Epeius shot his spear from a kneeling position at the on-coming Benomar; a powerful hit. The spearhead embedding itself in Benomar's shield, jolting the warrior for a moment, providing Epeius the instant he required to right himself.

Benomar attacked again, short sword pointed.

Epeius leapt aside like an agile cat, parrying the intended strike with his own weapon and catching the skin of Benomar's thigh in the process. First blood.

Benomar let out a savage yowl, feinted, side-stepped, grabbed the Greek by the edge of his breastplate, and hurled him to the ground.Epeius landed with a mighty thud, the impact bathing him in a cloud of sand.

Triumph presumed, Benomar raised his glinting sword.

Epeius! Epeius! Epeius!

No time to wipe his eyes, in blind desperation the Greek hurled his short sword like a stone. It glanced Benomar's right leg. Second blood.

The blow made Benomar miss his thrust, and again lose balance.

Without a weapon, Epeius pounced, landing a ferocious over-hand right to his astonished foe's forehead. The Greek's fists, still covered in *caestus*, left their mark.

Benomar cried in anguish, dropped his sword, and fell to his knees.

Epeius did not retreat. Blow after blow he threw, beating the dazed Benomar so brutally that blood spurts showered spectators, while hunks of skull and brain-matter scattered nearly as far.

Epeius! Epeius! Epeius! The crowd continued to goad him.

Finally exhausted, Epeius paused beside the now prostrate battered form that had been his opponent.

Epeius! Epeius! Epeius! The spectators roared with delight. Cassius leapt from his stool and pounded the wooden railing before him in wild elation. Marcellus slumped in his seat, focused on the mutilated mass that once was his servant.

Silver coins, open gate… The victor had begun to regain clarity. He reached inside his breastplate and removed the purse. Titus stood in the near exit transom smiling, motioning for Epeius to come.

Cassius burst out of the jubilant crowd to congratulate his savior. Before Epeius reached the escape tunnel he was ambushed from behind by the elated promoter, whom the gladiator mistook for a combatant. In one swift motion Epeius reached back and grabbed hold of the assumed attacker's throat, crushing the man's windpipe and discarding him like a sack of grain, before breaking into a sprint. *Chariot and ship await to take me home to Mica.*

Marcellus watched as Benomar's corpse was dragged by hook past Cassius's lifeless body. The general reached for the flagon of claret and poured himself another goblet of wine. He held it up, as if toasting the event. "I lost my best guard and nearly forfeited a fortune, had Cassius lived to collect his ten thousand *dinarlii*." Marcellus sipped the wine. "I must admit,61 today's games, for once, were not a bore."

THE END

SWEET DREAMS

www.ingramcontent.com/pod-product-compliance
Lightning Source LLC
Chambersburg PA
CBHW040958170626
46815CB00002B/63